Word List

Here is a list of words that might make it easier to read this book. You'll find them in boldface the first time they appear in the story.

reins	raynz
harnesses	HAR-ness-ez
knights	nyts
dreadful	DRED-ful
banquet	BANG-kwit
tapestry	TAP-is-tree
rescued	RES-kyood
legends	LEJ-undz
pillar	PIL-er
capture	KAP-cher
royalty	ROI-ul-tee
fortune	FOR-chun
solution	suh-LOO-shun

Barbie™

The Silver Deer

ISBN: 0-7172-8803-X

Grolier Books

Chapter One

It was a time of kings and queens and lords and ladies. Lady Barbie looked out the window of her horse-drawn carriage. She was riding through the English countryside with her friend Lady Midge.

"I have never been in this area before," Barbie told Midge. "It's so lovely."

"Indeed," Midge agreed.

Barbie and Midge were on their way to Cornwall. Out the window, they could see farmers working in the fields. They could also see cows grazing in the meadow nearby.

Soon dark clouds appeared in the sky. A strong wind began to blow, and rain began to fall. The horse leading the carriage gave a nervous whinny.

"Hush," Thomas, the coachman, said to the horse through the storm. "It will be all right. Come on, let's go."

The horse quieted down, and the carriage rolled along the dirt road. Barbie and Midge tried to relax, too.

Barbie said, "The rain makes everything look even prettier. See how it sparkles on the trees."

"Yes, it is pretty," said Midge. "But I hope it will not make us late for our visit."

Barbie nodded. They hoped to reach town before it got dark. They didn't have much farther to go. But the horse and carriage traveled slowly because the rain was making the road muddy.

"I am looking forward to seeing Lord

Henry and Lady Eve," said Barbie.

Midge agreed. "I am, too," she said. "It has been such a long time since we last saw them."

"Look!" Barbie cried. "We're nearing a forest!"

Barbie had often heard tales about strange and magical things happening in this forest. Now her heart beat faster as the carriage soon was surrounded by tall trees. The path was narrow, and they could hear the wind blowing through the trees.

"I wonder if those stories are true," Barbie thought.

The rain continued to pour down as the carriage rolled into a large clearing in the forest. Suddenly something silver darted past their window.

"What was that?" Barbie asked Midge.

The two young women looked out of the carriage window. They could hardly believe their eyes! There in the clearing stood a beautiful deer.

It was the color of silver!

"Look how its antlers shine!" cried Midge.

Barbie was also surprised. "I've never seen such a deer!"

The horse pulling their carriage also saw the deer. Suddenly the horse reared and whinnied in fright. Startled by the loud noise, the deer ran back through the trees. The horse's wet **reins** slipped through the coachman's hands. He tried to grab the reins again as the horse began to run out of control. But he couldn't reach them. Then the horse pulled the carriage right off the road!

"Oh, my!" Midge cried as the carriage rocked back and forth. The two friends gripped the doors and each other to steady themselves.

"Hold on!" shouted Barbie.

All at once, the carriage stopped with a jerk.

As soon as Barbie and Midge realized they were not hurt, Barbie called out to the coachman.

"Thomas, are you all right?"

Thomas came up to the window. "I apologize, my ladies," he said.

"What happened?" asked Midge.

"The horse got a bit frightened," Thomas explained. "Now it seems the carriage is stuck in a ditch."

"Oh, no!" the friends cried.

"Do not worry, my ladies," said Thomas. "I will do my best to pull us out."

"Is there anything we can do to help?" Barbie called out.

"Oh, no, my lady!" Thomas answered. "Please stay in the coach where it's dry."

"Thank you, Thomas," said Barbie.

The rain was coming down even harder now. Secretly Barbie thought the day was turning into quite an adventure! "Perhaps we will see that beautiful deer again," she said, turning to Midge.

"I hope so," Midge said. "I would love to get

a closer look at it."

"There was something magical about it," Barbie added. "Imagine! A deer the color of silver."

Outside, Thomas was pulling on the horse's reins. The carriage rocked a bit. But the wheels just sank deeper into the mud. The carriage was completely stuck!

Chapter Two

A little while later, a grand carriage stopped beside them. It was decorated with gold and pulled by four black horses. Even the horses had beautiful ribbons and **harnesses** on them.

A young woman leaned out the window. "Do you need help?" she asked them.

"Yes, thank you," Barbie replied. "I am Lady Barbie, and this is Lady Midge."

"I am Lady Anne," the woman told them. "Please come and wait inside my carriage."

One of the woman's coachmen held up a cape to keep the rain off Barbie and Midge. Then he helped them into the waiting carriage.

Once they were inside the carriage, Midge turned to Lady Anne. "Are you *the* Lady Anne?" she asked. "Daughter of Lord Richard?"

The woman nodded. "I am," she replied with a smile.

Barbie and Midge knew of Lord Richard. Everyone did. He ruled a large area of England and had many **knights**.

"I will take you to our castle until the storm passes," Anne told them.

"That's very kind of you," said Barbie.

"Yes," said Midge. "Thank you very much."

"James!" the woman called to the first coachman.

"Yes, my lady," James replied as he came to the window.

"Please unharness two horses," Anne instructed him. "They can help to pull out the ladies' carriage while we drive on. Afterward, you can lead their coachman back to the castle."

"As you wish," said James.

Before long, the carriage rumbled along the wet road with the three ladies inside. In such a horrible rainstorm, Barbie and Midge were very thankful that Anne had come along.

"Lady Anne must know this forest very well," Barbie thought. "I wonder if she knows about the mysterious deer we saw."

"This has been quite an adventure!" Barbie told Anne. "Back in the clearing, we saw the most unusual animal. It was a silver deer!"

But Anne didn't seem to hear Barbie. "Excuse me," she called to her other coachman, "please hurry along! These ladies will catch cold!"

Anne turned back to them and smiled. "Now, where were you headed?" she asked.

"To the home of friends in Cornwall," Midge replied. "Maybe you know them? Lord

Henry and Lady Eve?"

"Why, yes," Anne said. "Just last summer they visited us at our castle."

"Oh, how lovely," said Midge.

While Midge and Anne talked, Barbie looked out the window. Her mind kept wandering. She was thinking about the deer. She wanted to find out more about it.

Barbie turned to Anne. "Have you ever seen a silver deer in this forest?" she asked.

Suddenly Anne began to cough. "Pardon me," she said through another cough.

"Are you all right, Lady Anne?" asked Barbie, offering her a handkerchief.

Anne nodded. "Yes, thank you," she said. "This weather is rather awful, don't you think?"

"Yes, it's **dreadful**," said Midge.

Anne took a deep breath. "Now then," she said, "we can't have you traveling in all this rain. Why don't you stay at the castle tonight as my

10

guests? There is to be a **banquet** this evening. I'm sure you'd enjoy yourselves. Please stay."

Barbie and Midge looked at each other.

Midge smiled. "How can we refuse such a kind invitation?" she said.

"Yes," Barbie added. "We'd be honored."

"Wonderful!" said Anne. "We will be at the castle shortly."

Just then, Barbie saw another flash of silver. "Look!" she cried, looking out the window. "Isn't that the deer?"

"Oh, my!" Anne said as if Barbie hadn't said a word about the deer. "What about Lord Henry and Lady Eve? We must let them know you will be delayed and that you are safe. I will send a messenger to them as soon as we reach the castle."

Barbie turned back to Anne. "We don't want you to go to any trouble," Barbie said.

Anne patted Barbie's hand. "It's no trouble,"

she said. "No trouble at all."

When Barbie looked out the window again, the deer was gone.

Chapter Three

Soon they came to a town. The carriage continued on through narrow, twisting lanes. Small houses lined the muddy streets. As Barbie looked out the window, she could see a huge castle in the distance.

When they finally reached the castle, the coachman helped the three ladies out of the carriage. They hurried inside to get out of the rain. Their arrival was announced to Lord Richard.

"My dear child, where have you been?" cried Lord Richard. "I was getting worried."

"I'm sorry I'm so late, Father," replied Anne. "But I couldn't leave these poor travelers in the rain." She introduced Barbie and Midge to her father.

"It is a pleasure to meet you," Lord Richard said.

"Your daughter has been very kind to us," Barbie told him. Then she and Midge explained what had happened to their horse and carriage in the rain.

"What a day!" Lord Richard laughed. "It sounds as if you ladies need a pleasant evening to help you forget your troubles."

"That's very thoughtful of you," Barbie said.

"And I will have a message delivered to Lord Henry and Lady Eve letting them know you'll be staying here for the night," Lord Richard added.

"Thank you," said Midge.

Then Lord Richard waved to a servant.

"Please show our guests to their room."

"Yes, my lord," the servant replied.

"I'm sure you will want to rest after your long journey," Lord Richard said. "Please join us in the banquet hall later this evening for dinner."

"We look forward to it," said Midge.

"I hope you'll be feeling better by then, too," Barbie said to Anne.

Anne looked confused. "Better?" she asked.

"Your cough," Barbie reminded her.

"Yes, of course," Anne said quickly. "Thank you."

A servant led Barbie and Midge up a winding staircase. They entered a large room with a beautiful **tapestry** on the wall and a huge fireplace. Off to one side were two beautifully carved beds. Barbie walked to the window and saw a lush garden below.

"This is lovely," Barbie said. She thanked the servant, who nodded and left the room.

"Yes, it surely is," Midge replied. She walked to the fireplace to warm her hands. "Imagine our good fortune at being **rescued** by Lady Anne!"

"She is very nice," said Barbie, "but have you noticed that she avoids my questions about the silver deer?"

"Yes, I did notice," Midge agreed. "I thought that was strange myself. She always seems to change the subject."

Barbie got a twinkle in her eye. "You know, I have a feeling she knows something about this mysterious animal," she said.

"You could be right," said Midge.

"I think it's something she wants to keep a secret," added Barbie.

"How exciting this trip is becoming!" Midge cried.

"And how tiring," Barbie said. She yawned and lay down on one of the beds.

"It *has* been a long day," said Midge as she curled up on the other bed. Then they both took a short nap.

Chapter Four

Barbie and Midge were awakened by the
sound of a trumpet from somewhere in the castle.
It was time for the banquet!

Servants arrived carrying beautiful dresses
of velvet and silk. They helped Barbie and
Midge change into the long, flowing gowns.
When the ladies were ready, they were led into
the banquet hall for dinner.

"Look at this banquet room!" Midge
whispered to Barbie.

Along one wall there was a huge, glowing
fireplace. Enormous tapestries hung from the

other walls. Candles were everywhere. Anne and her father sat at a long table covered by a white tablecloth. The lords and ladies who were their guests sat on both sides of them. Everyone was beautifully dressed for the banquet. The women wore long, embroidered gowns and hats. The men wore fine coats with fur at the neck and wrists. Everyone wore shoes of silk and satin with long, pointy toes. Barbie and Midge were seated next to their two hosts.

Another trumpet sounded as other guests were seated. The meal was about to begin. The servants filed in carrying large trays piled with all sorts of foods.

"Thank you," Barbie told a servant as he filled her plate.

"Everything looks delicious!" said Midge.

A woman sitting next to Barbie introduced herself as Lady Sarah.

"I am pleased to meet you, Lady Sarah,"

said Barbie. "I am Lady Barbie. Is this your first visit to Lord Richard's castle?"

"No, I visit Lady Anne often," Lady Sarah replied. "How do you know her?"

"We met Lady Anne today while traveling through the forest," said Barbie. "She helped us when our carriage became stuck in a ditch."

"Oh, my!" said Lady Sarah.

"I loved riding through the forest, though," said Barbie. "It seems so magical, don't you think?"

"Yes," replied Lady Sarah. "It is quite an unusual place."

Barbie smiled. "In fact, riding along today, we saw the most amazing deer," she said.

"Ladies," Anne said, interrupting, "is everything to your liking?"

"Why, yes," the ladies replied. "Thank you."

"Good," said Anne. "There is more in store after the feast." Anne went on to tell them about the games to be played later.

While the dishes were being cleared, Midge leaned over to Barbie. "Lady Anne did it again!" she whispered. "You started to talk about the deer, and she changed the subject."

"I know," Barbie whispered back. "We've got to find out what's going on!"

After the meal, servants brought in games and tables for chess. Another trumpet sounded, and a singer entered the hall. Everyone gathered close as he took out his lute. He strummed its strings and began to sing:

I love the merry spring weather
That is coming here so soon.
The flowers grow so quickly,
By the light of the sun and the moon.
The forest is so cool and dark,
Its paths roam far and near.
Who knows what magic it does have,
Who knows of the silver deer?

Barbie leaned over to Midge. "The singer must be talking about the deer in the forest!" she said in a quiet voice.

"You're right!" Midge replied.

"*Legends old and legends new*," the singer continued.

"Please stop!" Anne suddenly commanded.

The singer stopped playing and the room became silent.

"I am sorry," Anne said gently. "But I grow tired of that song. Please, let us hear a love song instead!"

Then Anne nodded toward Barbie and Midge. "Our guests will surely enjoy that more," she said.

Barbie gave a polite smile. Secretly she wanted to hear the rest of the song and the legend of the deer. But it would be impolite to say so now.

The singer bowed and agreed to Anne's

request. Then he sang of a young man searching for his true love.

For the moment, Barbie and Midge forgot about the deer. They enjoyed themselves as the songs and games continued long into the night.

Chapter Five

Finally it was time for bed. Barbie and Midge thanked their hosts for a wonderful evening. Then they made their way to their bedroom.

Inside, Midge walked to the window and looked outside. "I'm not tired at all," she told Barbie.

Barbie grinned. "Neither am I," she said. "Why don't we go for a walk in the garden? It looks as if it's turned into a lovely night now that the rain has stopped."

They tiptoed downstairs. The castle was

dark and silent.

"I guess everyone has gone to bed," said Midge.

"I think this is the way to the garden," Barbie said. She and Midge started down a long hallway.

Suddenly they heard footsteps and loud voices coming down the hall toward them.

Barbie jumped back and pulled Midge behind a **pillar**. "Shh!" Barbie whispered.

Soldiers raced down the hall past them.

"Hurry! Lord Richard is waiting for us," said one of the soldiers. "We are needed to get ready for a **capture**!"

And just as quickly as they had come, the soldiers were gone.

"I wonder what that was all about," said Midge.

But before Barbie could answer, they heard voices once again.

"It sounds like a woman," Barbie whispered to Midge.

Moving slowly, they peeked around the pillar.

"It's Lady Anne!" they whispered to each other.

"Thank you," Anne was saying to her coachman, James. "Thank you for your loyal service."

James bowed deeply.

Anne continued, "Please ride into the forest tonight. Perhaps you can locate the silver deer and find a safe hiding place for him."

"Yes, my lady," said James, bowing again. He turned and began walking down the hall.

"The deer again!" Midge whispered. "That must be the capture the soldiers were talking about!"

Barbie and Midge waited until they thought it was safe. Then they tiptoed away from the pillar. But, to their surprise, they bumped right

into Anne!

"Oh!" Barbie said, surprised. "Please excuse us."

Anne wiped away a tear from her eye. "Forgive me," she answered. "I am not in the habit of crying in front of guests."

"Is there anything we can do?" Barbie asked.

Anne sighed. "I'm sure you heard me talking to James." She paused a moment. Then she looked at Barbie and Midge closely. "You *did* see him, didn't you?"

"Your coachman?" asked Midge. "Yes, we did."

Anne smiled. "No, not James. My one true love. The silver deer in the forest," she said quietly.

Barbie gasped. She was certain there was something magical about that deer!

"The deer is really a young man," Anne

explained, "a young man I want to marry. But now he is under a spell."

"A spell!" Barbie cried.

"Oh, please! You must tell us the whole story!" said Midge.

"There is an old legend about a silver deer," said Anne. "And that legend puts my love in danger."

Barbie leaned forward. "Please go on!" she said.

"Let's sit where we can be comfortable and no one can hear us," said Anne. "Then I will start from the beginning."

Chapter Six

Barbie and Midge followed Anne into a room with a large fireplace. They took seats near the fire and warmed their hands.

"The young man's name is William," Lady Anne began. "He is a poor shoemaker. We love each other with all our hearts and wish to marry. But I am not allowed to marry anyone who is not **royalty**."

"How sad!" said Barbie.

"One year ago, on the first day of spring, William and I were walking by the River of Dreams. We saw a deer the color of silver," Anne told them. "We had heard tales of this deer and its powers before. But we were surprised when it spoke to us!"

"Oh, my!" exclaimed Barbie and Midge.

"The deer said that he was the King of the Forest," Anne continued. "He told us how he longed to be human, even for just a short time. He wanted to do all the things that animals can't do."

"Like what?" Midge wondered.

Anne smiled. "The deer reminded William and me of all the wonderful things that humans can do that animals can't. We can sing and dance. We can learn new things. We can make choices and even fall in love."

"How romantic," sighed Midge.

Anne blushed and continued her story. "William and I told the deer about our wish to marry and my father's objections. We told him that humans don't always get to make choices

they like," said Anne.

"Then the deer stared straight at William and said, 'Let us trade places for one year. In return, I will help your wish come true.' "

"Amazing!" Barbie exclaimed.

"The deer promised to make William a prince by giving him a crown of silver after the year was up. I begged William not to do it. But he was sure this was the only way we could be together," Anne said.

Barbie nodded. "Then William would be royalty."

"Yes," replied Anne. "Early the next morning, I heard a noise outside my window. When I stepped out onto my balcony, I saw a silver deer below. It bowed and then raced off toward the woods. I knew it was William saying good-bye."

"How sad!" cried Midge.

"Now the year is almost over. Tomorrow

will be the first day of spring," Anne explained. "In order for William to become human again, he must drink from the River of Dreams at sunset. Then the spell will be broken, and he will be a prince."

"Then you should be happy," said Midge.

"But right now William is in danger," Anne replied.

"The capture!" Barbie gasped. "Your father has called for the capture of the deer! Oh, it's all my fault! I spotted the deer and tried to speak of it. I'm so sorry!"

Anne shook her head. "Don't worry," she told Barbie. "My father did not hear it from you. I stopped you each time you spoke. But your coachman has told many people about the deer."

"Oh, no!" Barbie said.

"It doesn't matter now," Anne said quickly. "Chances are the deer would have been seen by someone else. And now, because of the legend, my father will stop at nothing to catch William."

"What *is* the legend?" Midge asked. "What does it say?"

"It says, if you capture the silver deer unharmed, you and your kingdom will be blessed with good **fortune**," explained Anne.

"No wonder your father wants the silver deer for his own!" Barbie said.

"Yes," Anne replied. "My only hope is for William to be at the River of Dreams at sunset tomorrow for the change to occur. But if William is captured before he is human again, I shall lose him forever!"

"We must do something!" said Midge.

"Yes, I know," said Anne. "But what?"

"Don't worry," Barbie said. "We'll think of something!"

Anne was thankful for the help of her new friends. But would they be able to come up with a plan in time?

Chapter Seven

Barbie woke up early the next morning to the sound of birds chirping outside the window.

"The first day of spring," she said to herself. She thought maybe a walk in the garden would help her to come up with a plan to stop the capture. Midge was still asleep, so Barbie dressed quietly and went outside.

The sun shone brightly. Barbie was happy the rain had gone away. All around the castle, people were coming and going in every direction. Servants rushed back and forth. Young men saddled horses. Soldiers prepared themselves for the capture. Women brought out baskets of food. Music played and people were laughing. All were happy, thinking about the good fortune the capture of the silver deer would bring them.

Lord Richard was eager for the search for the deer to begin. "We will separate into groups," he shouted. "We will comb the forest and find that silver deer!"

Walking among all the people, Barbie spotted Lady Anne's coachman, James.

"That's it!" thought Barbie. "I know just what to do!"

When she reached James, Barbie told him of her plan. He quickly agreed.

Barbie went inside the castle to find Midge. When she found her, they both hurried to Anne's bedroom. Barbie saw how sad and worried Anne looked.

"James couldn't find William in the forest last night to warn him," Anne said.

"Don't worry," Barbie said gently. "I think I have a **solution** to your problem."

"That's wonderful!" cried Anne. "But right now we had better go to the window. My father is expecting us to send him off."

The three young women could barely stand still as they waited for Lord Richard and his soldiers to leave.

At last they heard Lord Richard give a great shout outside Anne's window. "Now let the search begin!" his voice boomed.

Barbie, Midge, and Anne waved out the window to wish the men good luck.

"In my heart, this is one time I can't wish my father good luck," said Anne tearfully.

Barbie leaned a little farther out the window. She could see James the coachman below. She waved her handkerchief in his direction. When James caught sight of Barbie, he nodded and headed to the stables.

As soon as Lord Richard and his men had gone, Barbie turned to her friends. "I have asked James to leave three saddled horses for us by the East Gate," she told them. "Only we know that William must be at the River of Dreams by sunset. We will go on our own to meet him. With any luck, we will find him on our way."

Anne turned to Barbie and gasped. "Oh, Barbie, that is a marvelous idea!" she exclaimed. "But the river is a long ride away."

"Then let's get started! There's not a moment to lose!" declared Barbie.

Barbie, Midge, and Anne put on their cloaks and hurried to their horses. The women were careful to travel in the opposite direction from Lord Richard's soldiers. Galloping at top speed, they raced along the forest paths hoping to see the silver deer.

But as the day went on they saw no sign of the magical creature. It was almost sunset by the time they neared the river.

"Hurry," called Anne, "we're almost there." But just then, Anne's cloak became caught on a low-hanging branch.

"Oh, dear!" she cried. They all stopped to help Anne untangle her cloak.

Anne looked at her friends, her eyes filling with tears. "We can't lose any more time. We must find William before my father does!"

"Don't worry," said Barbie. "I think I can see a river up ahead." Barbie gave her horse a gentle tap, and the ladies rode on.

"Is this the River of Dreams?" Barbie shouted to Anne.

"Yes, it is!" Anne called back. "And this is the same spot where William and I first met the silver deer."

They slowed their horses to a stop and dismounted.

"I don't see William," said Midge as she

looked around.

"Neither do I," Anne worried. "I hope he hasn't been captured."

"It's not quite sunset," said Barbie. "I'm sure he'll be here."

Anne sighed. "How will I ever thank you both for all your help?" she said.

"When you and William are together, that will be thanks enough," said Barbie.

Suddenly Barbie heard rustling behind her. She turned around quickly.

"Look!" Barbie cried. "It's the silver deer!"

Sure enough, the deer was standing right before them!

"William!" Lady Anne cried with joy.

"It's really him!" Midge declared.

The deer came up to Anne and began to nuzzle her hand.

"It's all right," Anne whispered. "It's all right, my love."

Midge glanced toward the sky. "It's almost sunset," she said.

The deer nuzzled Anne's hand again. "Yes, that's right," said Anne. "It is almost time for you to drink from the River of Dreams."

Just then the booming sound of horses' hooves broke the silence. Lord Richard and his men burst into the forest clearing. Lord Richard pulled on his horse's reins to stop. His soldiers were right behind him.

Chapter Eight

"Anne!" Lord Richard shouted to his daughter.

"Father!" she replied.

"What are you doing here, Anne?" asked Lord Richard. Then he saw the silver deer next to her. He jumped off his horse and ran up to them.

"At last! This rare creature will finally be mine!" Lord Richard cried. "And good fortune will come to our castle."

"I care nothing of fortune, Father," Anne cried. She stepped between him and the deer.

"Move aside, Daughter. You ladies should

all be at the castle. Why are you here?" he asked.

"My lord, we beg your pardon," said Barbie softly. "But we are here as friends of your daughter."

"What is this all about?" Lord Richard demanded angrily.

"I beg you," Barbie pleaded, "please do not capture this animal."

"Why not?" Lord Richard asked.

Midge pointed to the deer. "Look at him. He is the color of silver," she said. "Don't you see that this deer is magical?"

"Of course," Lord Richard told her. "That is what the legend says, and that is why I must have it."

"But there is another legend from *our* part of England," said Barbie, thinking quickly. "A different one. It says that true happiness will only come to those who treat all living things with kindness and respect."

The forest was getting dark. The fading sunlight made the river glow orange.

Lord Richard looked at the deer. Then he looked at the ladies. "I barely know you," he told Barbie and Midge. "Yet you expect me to believe you?"

"Yes," Barbie said. "You must."

"You say that I will be given happiness for leaving the deer alone," Lord Richard said. "But what could make one happier than fortune?"

Barbie smiled at Anne and the deer.

"I will show you," she said. "Look into the eyes of your daughter. Then ask yourself this question: Isn't her happiness worth more than any great fortune?"

Lord Richard walked over to his daughter and put his hand under her chin. He gazed at her. A tear fell from her eye. Then Anne went to the river and scooped up a handful of water. She held it out to the deer, who drank it.

Suddenly a streak of light came down from the sky. Surprised, everyone backed away. The light surrounded the deer. For a moment, he even disappeared inside it!

Then, all at once, the light went away. The deer was gone. In its place stood a prince. He was wearing a cape and a shining crown of silver!

"William!" Anne cried.

"My love," the prince replied. He clasped her hand and brought it to his heart. "We are together again."

Lord Richard stared at the young man. "Who is this young man standing before me?"

"It is William," Anne replied. "My one true love."

Anne explained to her father how William had exchanged places with the deer for one year so that he could become a prince.

Lord Richard was touched by the young man's love of his daughter and the sacrifice he

had made for their future. He offered his hand
to Prince William. "Welcome to our family."

"Is it because I now wear a crown that you
welcome me?" asked Prince William.

"Your crown is only a small part of the
reason," Lord Richard told him. "You have
shown your love for my daughter by giving up
a year of your life. You have risked countless
dangers. I would be honored to call you *son*."

"Now you can be married!" Barbie said
to Anne.

Anne smiled. "That's right," she said. "And
all thanks to my two new friends."

Barbie and Midge smiled happily as Lady
Anne joined Prince William on her horse.

Anne turned to her friends. Then, with a
twinkle in her eyes, she said, "Well, it seems
that you won't get to Cornwall after all."

"What do you mean, Lady Anne?" wondered
a confused Midge.

"Well, Lord Henry and Lady Eve will surely come here to be at our wedding," replied Anne. "And of course you both must stay and be my bridesmaids."

"We'd be honored," said Barbie.

"Oh, yes," said Midge. Then Midge looked at Barbie. "Who knew this trip would lead to a royal wedding?"

Barbie laughed. "I guess you could say that true love can be found in all sorts of places," she said. "Even on the road to Cornwall!"